HEARING

Anita Ganeri

Smart Apple Media

Published by Smart Apple Media
P.O. Box 1329
Mankato, MN 56002

Printed in the United States of America,
at Corporate Graphics in North Mankato, Minnesota.

Designed and illustrated by Guy Callaby
Edited by Mary-Jane Wilkins

Library of Congress Cataloging-in-Publication Data

Ganeri, Anita, 1961-
  Hearing / by Anita Ganeri.
    p. cm. -- (Senses)
  Includes bibliographical references and index.
  Summary: "In simple language, explains how the ears work
to help us hear. Describes how the parts of the ear take in light
and how the nerves in the ear send messages to the brain to tell
us what we hear"--Provided by publisher.
  ISBN 978-1-59920-851-0 (hardcover, library bound : alk.
paper)
  1. Hearing--Juvenile literature. 2. Ear--Juvenile literature. I.
Title.
  QP462.2.G36 2013
  612.8'5--dc23
                    2012004122

Picture acknowledgements
l = left, r = right, c = center, t = top, b = bottom
page 1 iStockphoto/Thinkstock; 2 Digital Vision/Thinkstock,
3t Sergey Fedenko/Shutterstock, 3c Gorilla/Shutterstock,
3b Gelpi/Shutterstock; 4 Jupiterimages/Thinkstock;
6 Hemera/Thinkstock; 7 ingret/Shutterstock; 8c IrinaK/
Shutterstock, b iStockphoto/Thinkstock; 9 ravl/Shutterstock;
10 Zoonar/Thinkstock; 11 iStockphoto/Thinkstock;
13 iStockphoto/Thinkstock; 14 iStockphoto/Thinkstock;
15 Stockbyte/Thinkstock; 16 Ilike/Shutterstock;
17 iStockphoto/Thinkstock; 18 Sportlibrary/Shutterstock;
19 Jupiterimages/Thinkstock; 20 auremar/Shutterstock;
21 andras_csontos/Shutterstock; 22c iStockphoto/Thinkstock,
b Johan Swanepoel/Shutterstock; 23 borkiss/Shutterstock;
image beneath folios Jupiterimages/Thinkstock
Cover: Thinkstock

DAD0506
042012
9 8 7 6 5 4 3 2 1

Contents

Hear, Hear

What happens when you listen to music? What sounds can you hear?

You use your ears to listen to someone playing the guitar.

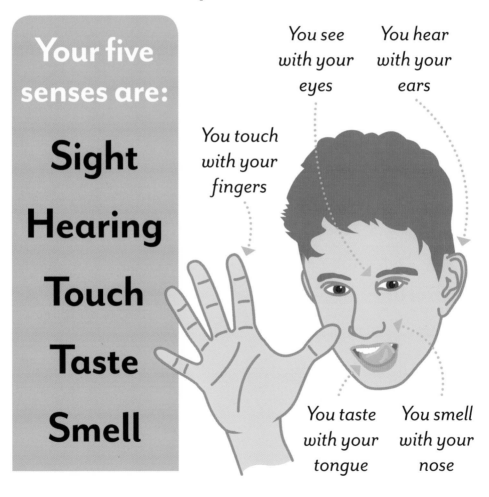

Hearing is one of your senses. Your senses tell you about the world around you.

Your five senses are:

Sight

Hearing

Touch

Taste

Smell

You see with your eyes

You hear with your ears

You touch with your fingers

You taste with your tongue

You smell with your nose

What Can You Hear?

There are lots of different sounds. Some sounds are loud, such as a jet plane taking off.

Some sounds are **soft**, such as a cat purring or a person whispering.

What Are Sounds?

Sounds make the air wobble. High sounds make the air wobble very quickly.

A mouse makes a high sound when it squeaks.

Dogs can pick up sounds that are too high for you to hear.

Low sounds

make the air wobble slowly.

How Do You Hear?

You hear sounds with your two ears. Your earflaps catch the sounds.

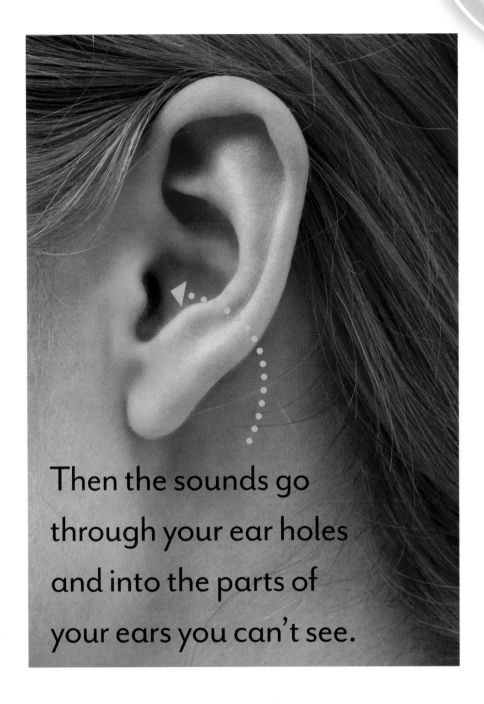

Then the sounds go through your ear holes and into the parts of your ears you can't see.

Inside Your Ears

The sounds go down a tube
to some thin skin, called your
ear drum. They make
it wobble.

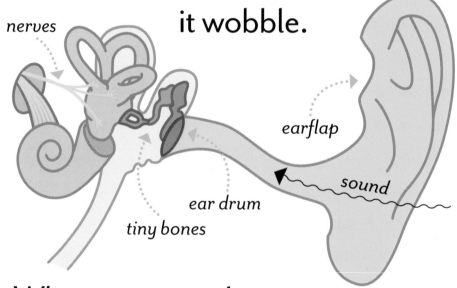

nerves

earflap

sound

ear drum

tiny bones

When your ear drum
wobbles, it makes three
tiny ear bones wobble, too.

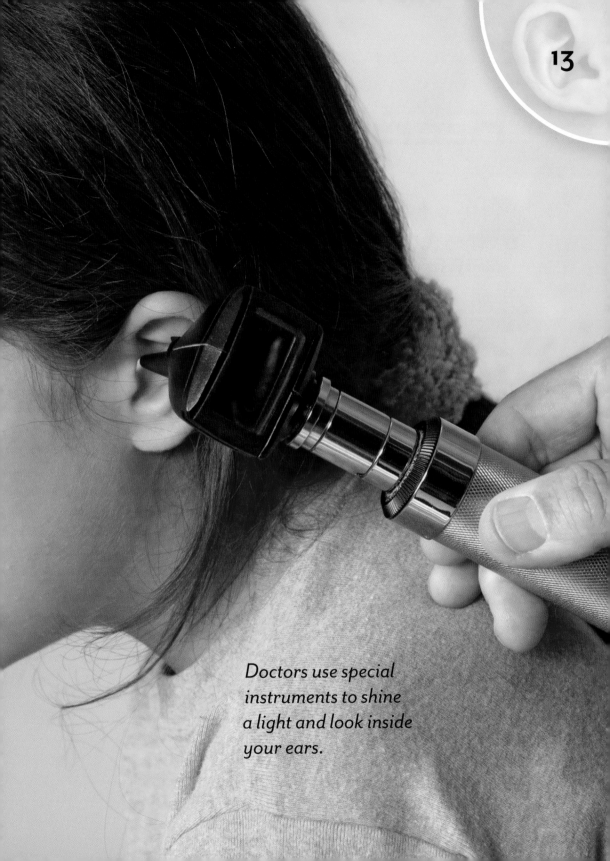

Doctors use special instruments to shine a light and look inside your ears.

Hearing Messages

The wobbling goes deeper inside your ears where there is liquid and hairy nerves.

The hairs deep inside your ears are a bit like the bristles on a toothbrush.

The liquid wobbles and pulls on the hairs. The hairs send **messages** to your brain to tell you what you can hear.

Your brain tells you what the person on the phone is saying to you.

Two Ears

Why do you have two ears? It helps to tell you where sounds are coming from.

Sounds hit one ear before the other, so the wobbles are stronger in the first ear.

*Two ears help you
to hear sounds all
around you.*

In a Spin

Apart from hearing, your ears also help you to balance and to spin around quickly.

Nerves send messages to your brain. Your brain tells your body what to do so that you don't fall over.

If you spin round, then stop, you feel dizzy. This is because the liquid inside your ears keeps swirling about.

Being Deaf

Some people cannot hear very well. People who can't hear are deaf.

Loud sounds can hurt your ears and stop them working properly.

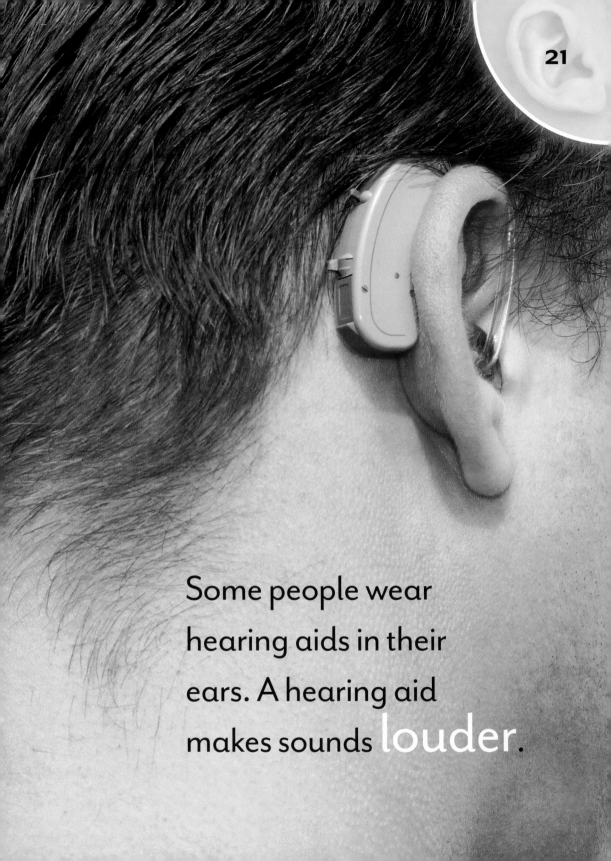

Some people wear
hearing aids in their
ears. A hearing aid
makes sounds louder.

Hearing Facts

The tiny bones in your ears are the smallest bones in your body. They are about the same size as grains of rice.

This shows just how small your ear bones are!

African elephants have the biggest ears of any animal. Their earflaps are as big as a single bedsheet.

You have yellowish wax inside your ears to catch tiny specks of dirt and dust.

Some animals, such as rabbits and cats, can move their ears to help them catch sounds.

Useful Words

ear drum
A thin piece of skin that stretches across the tube inside your ear.

earflaps
The parts of your ears you can see on the outside of your head.

nerves
Thin, long wires inside your body that carry messages between your body and brain.

sounds
Another word for the noises you can hear.

Index